KU-515-297

Shaun the Sheep™ MOVIE
SMALL SHEEP, BIG CITY

WALKER
ENTERTAINMENT

Every day on Mossy Bottom Farm is the same.

The cockerel crows,
the Farmer tears a page
from the calendar, and
Shaun slowly wakes up.

The Farmer reaches
for the day's schedule.

Today is a shearing day.
That's different, but it's not fun.

The sheep are bored. Shaun is bored.
HE WANTS A DAY OFF.

Shaun has a plan. Instead of going into the meadow, the sheep take turns to jump over the gate.

They jump again and again.

The Farmer counts the sheep.

He counts and counts and soon falls asleep.

TIME FOR FUN!

The sleeping Farmer is put to bed in the caravan, and the Flock have a party in his house. They watch movies and eat pizza and ice cream and other snacks.

But the fun doesn't last. When Bitzer finds out, he makes the Flock go to the caravan to wake the Farmer.

But the caravan rolls down the hill, toward the Big City, with the Farmer still inside!

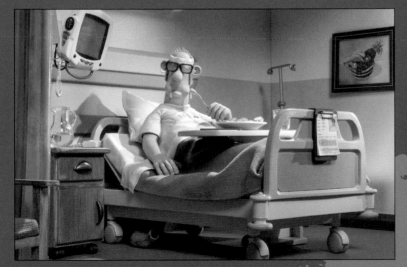

Along the way, the Farmer gets bumped on the head. He wakes up in the hospital and can't remember who he is.

Back at the farm,
Shaun is upset.
WHERE IS THE FARMER?
Is he coming back?

Shaun makes a poster.
Then he takes the bus
to the Big City
to find the Farmer.

Shaun has to hide
on the bus.

What does Shaun find when he gets there?

THE FLOCK!

They have followed him.

Sheep don't really belong in the Big City, so they
have to be careful not to get caught by Officer Trumper.

He runs the Animal Containment Centre,
and he wants to lock them up.

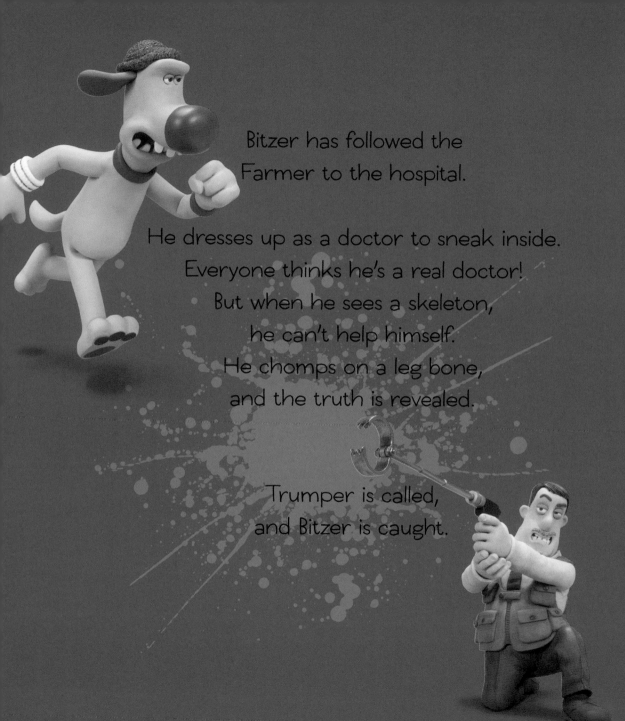

Bitzer has followed the
Farmer to the hospital.

He dresses up as a doctor to sneak inside.
Everyone thinks he's a real doctor!
But when he sees a skeleton,
he can't help himself.
He chomps on a leg bone,
and the truth is revealed.

Trumper is called,
and Bitzer is caught.

The sheep go into a restaurant.
They are dressed like people,
but they don't know how to act like people.

Timmy loves the restaurant. He eats sweets from the dessert trolley. Shaun's jumper gets caught on the trolley and unravels, and everyone can see that he's a sheep.

RUN!

The rest of the Flock escapes, but Shaun isn't so lucky. Trumper catches him. He is taken to the Containment Centre. Bitzer is already there.

The Farmer runs away from the hospital.

Wandering around the Big City,
he sees a pair of hair clippers in a hair salon.

HMMM, he thinks. Something about them looks familiar.

He goes inside, grabs the clippers,
and shears a man waiting there.
Everyone is shocked, but
the man loves his new haircut.
The Farmer is a hair-cutting star!

The Flock try to rescue Shaun and Bitzer
from the Containment Centre.
They pull and pull and finally, with Shirley's help,
they tear down the wall. But there's a problem.
It's the wrong wall.

Shaun and Bitzer make their own escape plan,
and soon they are free.

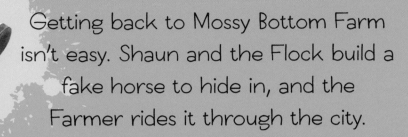

Getting back to Mossy Bottom Farm isn't easy. Shaun and the Flock build a fake horse to hide in, and the Farmer rides it through the city.

They find the caravan and hitch it to a bus, which speeds them all back to the farm.

The sheep don't know it, but Trumper has come along for the ride! He tries to push the Flock off a cliff using the Farmer's tractor. But the Farmer gets his memory back just in time and sends Trumper into the manure pile.

POOH!

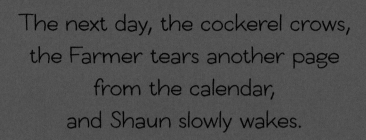

The next day, the cockerel crows,
the Farmer tears another page
from the calendar,
and Shaun slowly wakes.

But then the Farmer
crumples up the schedule
and tosses it away.

Finally—
A DAY OFF!

First published 2015 by Walker Entertainment
An imprint of Walker Books Ltd
87 Vauxhall Walk, London SE11 5HJ

2 4 6 8 10 9 7 5 3 1

© and TM Aardman Animations Limited and STUDIOCANAL S.A. 2015.
All rights reserved.
Shaun the Sheep (word mark) and the character Shaun the Sheep are trademarks used
under licence from Aardman Animations Limited

No part of this book may be reproduced, transmitted or stored in an information retrieval system
in any form or by any means, graphic, electronic or mechanical, including photocopying, taping and recording,
without prior written permission from the publisher.

This book was typeset in Boudoir.

Printed in Slovakia

British Library Cataloguing in Publication Data:
A catalogue record for this book is available from the British Library

ISBN 978-1-4063-6212-1

www.walker.co.uk